I0712684

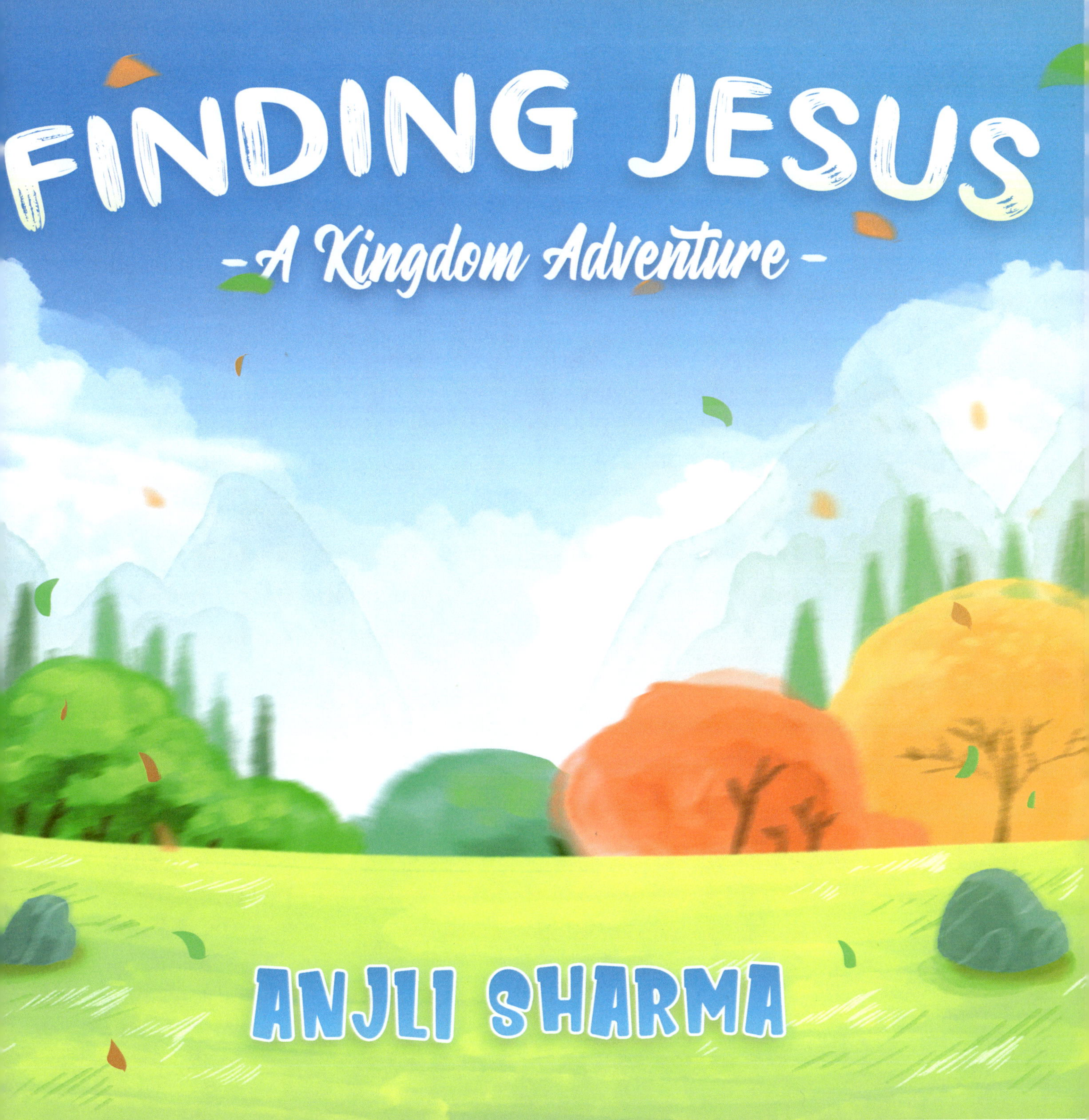

FINDING JESUS
-A Kingdom Adventure -
ANJLI SHARMA

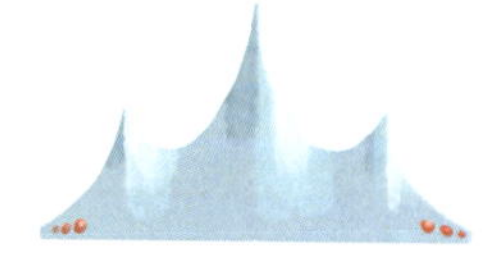

2020 Anjli Sharma

ISBN: 979-8-695-87109-8 (paperback)
ISBN: 978-0-578-78309-3 (hardcover)

First Edition Book, October 2020

Book cover design, illustration, editing, and interior layout by:
1000 Storybooks

www.1000storybooks.com

Dedication

I dedicate *Finding Jesus* to God. He gave me the vision of writing this children's book, and it has been such a blessing. This book is also dedicated to children everywhere who are looking for someone to comfort and encourage them when life gets tough. May they meet the Jesus written about in these pages.

Habakkuk 2:2 (NIV) "Then the Lord replied: 'Write down the revelation and make it plain on tablets so that a herald may run with it.'"

Once upon a time there was a beautiful Indian princess named Riya who lived in a far away palace in Rajasthan, India. She was engaged to marry a handsome Indian prince named Raj TOMORROW!

She had been planning her wedding with Raj for a whole year! There were so many flowers. Every color you can imagine! There was gold and shining emeralds hanging from the ceiling, a long red carpet, and even an elephant with colorful paint on his face!

She was so excited. How would she sleep?!

When she awoke the next morning there was a note laying right next to her pillow. Her hands were shaking as she ripped the letter open to discover the day's first big surprise!

It was from Prince Raj, hooray!

She opened it up, and she couldn't believe what it said. Her heart sank down into her toes...

My Dearest Riya,
I am so sorry, but i will not be marrying you today.
It's not you, it's me.
-Raj

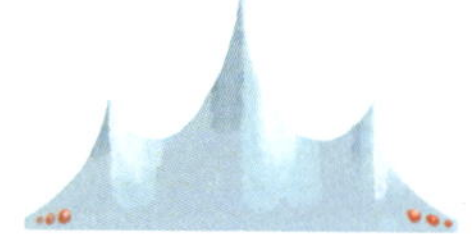

Riya felt her heart break in half. It hurt so bad she thought it would explode!

She rushed all over town to ask different people to help heal her broken heart, but none of the sorcerers, witches, or wizards were able to help her.

She ran into a dark alley, sat down in the dirt, put her face in her hands, and filled them with tears.

Worst day ever!

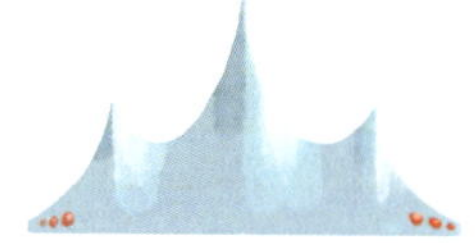

She needed something to heal her hurting heart, so she decided to pack her bags and leave the palace without saying a word to her family.

Outside of the palace walls, Para, her magical white unicorn awaited her. Princess Riya jumped on and together they rode! Her heart was still sad, and she had no peace.

She didn't pay attention to where Para was taking her. She just kept her arms wrapped tightly around Para's neck as she galloped for days and nights through strange lands.

On the morning of the third day, Princess Riya woke up when a big splash of water hit her in the face. Para was swimming out to a beautiful Paradise Island. Unicorns are amazing! It looked like a perfect place to rest.

Para felt very thirsty, so she drank some water from the sea.

Princess Riya jumped off Para's back onto the beach and saw the name JESUS written on the sand, and immediately she wondered what it meant. Was it the name of a local tribe? Was it the name of the beach? A type of food? She had no idea, but she was curious to find out. There seemed to be something quite magical about it.

JESUS

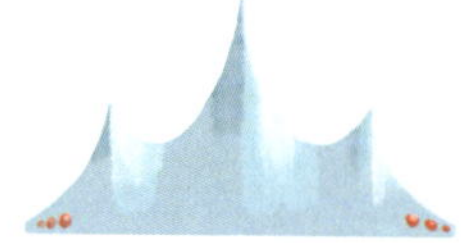

Riya and Para continued on their journey.

 Next they arrived in Jumbo Jungle where there were lots of trees and fruits. Princess Riya grabbed the biggest, juiciest apple she had ever seen, but just as she was about to eat it, she saw the name JESUS again! This time it was written on a leaf.

She wondered again, What is JESUS?

Again, she felt a strange, warm feeling in her chest that made the pain better for a few minutes. She had to find more about Jesus to cure her broken heart!

JESUS

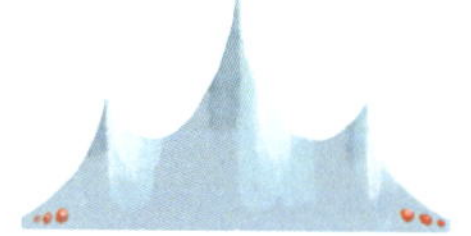

Princess Riya and Para continued searching for this Jesus thing and soon they came to the Dangerous Desert.

 There they saw camels walking by. Princess Riya leaned over and whispered to Para.

"Where do you think they are going?"

So Princess Riya decided to approach an old man on one of the camels.

"Hi, um, excuse me! Where are you going, Sir, and, um, what's with the camels?"

He answered with a warm smile, "We are going to see the Prince of Peace, Jesus. These camels have boxes of gifts for him."

"Perfect! That's exactly what, I mean who, I was hoping to find. Prince of Peace! Music to my ears! Can I come with you?"
"Of course my dear, follow us."

Princess Riya and Para followed the old man and the camels, and they arrived in a town with a lot of lights, houses, and a maze of dusty streets.

She saw people shopping in the streets and wondered how much farther the camels were going.

After days of riding on a unicorn's back her heart wasn't the only thing hurting!

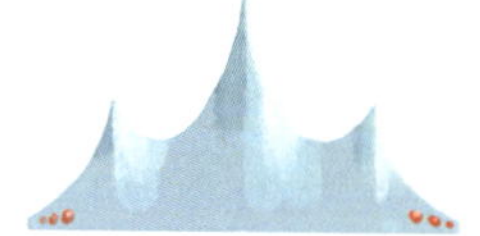

The old man stopped at a house full of lights and said to Princess Riya,

"This is where Jesus lives. He lives here in this house."

Princess Riya was very excited, so she put on her best friendly face to meet him.

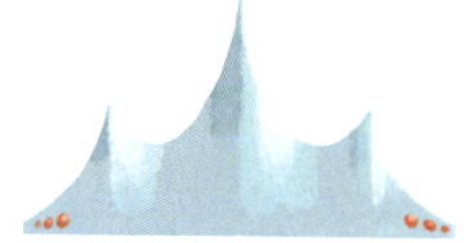

She saw him eating dinner with his family. Jesus noticed her, put his fork down and said, "Hello there girl. Have you come to see me?"

"Yes Jesus. I need serious help."

Jesus asked, "How can I help you?"

"Well there was this guy. A prince and all. And I was supposed to get married. But I woke up and there was a note. And, and... Well I totally have a broken heart., Can you fix it?"

Jesus was calm. He simply stretched out his arm with his fingers slightly apart. Riya got quiet and just looked up into his eyes. It was like looking up at the stars on a dark night. And in a gentle but strong voice he said,

"Be healed, my child. You will now be free to carry on!"

Princess Riya felt warmth in her chest and felt her heart come back together whole and then open up like a butterfly spreading its wings. Then she spread her arms up to the sky and said,

"There is no one like Him! He is the Lord Jesus that has healed my heart and set it free!"

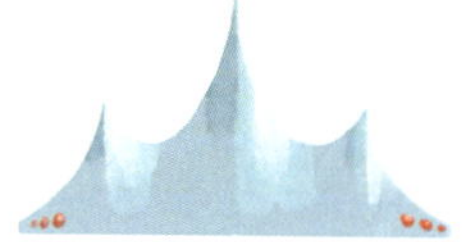

Princess Riya thanked Jesus and rode Para back to the palace immediately to tell her entire royal family about Jesus.

They thought she was crazy.

She and Para left the palace again, because her family didn't want to believe in Jesus. She left to go back to the village to see Jesus a second time, only to hear people in the village talking about how Jesus had died while she was gone!

Princess Riya felt her heart breaking again.

Riya and Para raced to Jesus's home to ask his family what happened. They said He died on a cross, but three days later the tomb was found empty. He rose from the dead on the third day! Jesus was alive again!

She was so excited to hear that Princess Riya prayed for Jesus to heal her once more.

After praying, Princess Riya found Jesus and his peace a second time. From then on, she lived praying to Jesus and telling other people about how Jesus restored, healed, and brought her everlasting love.

S Is For...
Serial Killers

Printed in Oliver Springs, Tennessee, United States of America
Library of Congress Control Number: 9798988033820

Description: Crimson Cult Media, 2023 | 32 pages of 4-color illustrations. | Series: Little Lestrange. | Audience. Adult. | Summary: Little Lestrange learns about the dark side of history by examining notorious serial killers from A to Z.
Identifiers: Library of Congress Control Numbers: 2023947630
|ISBN: 979-8-9880338-2-0
Subjects: FICTION_HORROR, WIT AND HUMOR| Picture Books.

To all the True Crime fanatics out there, this one's for you! I dedicate this book to those who have spent countless hours reading and watching *those* documentaries, consuming unsolved mysteries, and who can't seem to resist a true crime or spooky podcast (like Moths to the Flame!) To those who have a morbid fascination with the darker side of humanity or who have scared their friends and family with an extensive knowledge of murder cases. To those who have ever wondered if they missed their calling as a detective or forensic scientist. This book is for you, the true crime aficionados...the ones who know that most of the time the truth is stranger than any fiction we could ever create. May you find comfort in your obsession (because dammit, if they ever kidnapped one of us we'd try our best to leave a trail of DNA behind...right!?)

May your dreams (and life!) never be haunted by the monsters we learn about, and remember to always lock your doors at night!

-Lady Marie Lestrange

Blood is red, their lips are blue,
Aileen Wuornos had a job to do.
She shot seven men, "that they let her get."
She claimed self-defense, and that's no threat.

A is for Aileen Wuornos

Life: 1956-2002
Execution: Lethal Injection
State: Florida
Victims: 7
Criminal Penalty: 6 Death Sentences

B is for David Berkowitz

Life: 1953-Present
Imprisoned at: Shawangunk CXXF
State: New York
Victims: 6 killed, 11 wounded
Criminal Penalty: 6 Death Sentences

"I am a monster. I am the Son of Sam."

David Berkowitz, Son of
Sam,
wrote letters that cause a
media jam.
His antics once taunted the
police and press,
and now *thinks* his art
brings happiness.

Carl Panzram, a criminal so vile,
committed crimes that encourages bile.
He killed and assaulted with no remorse.
Died in 1930, by hanging, of course.

"I wish you all had one neck and that I had my hands on it."

C is for Carl Panzram

Life: 1891-1930
Execution: Hanging
Location: USA/Portugal
Victims: 5 confirmed, 21 confessed, 100+ suspected
Criminal Penalty: Death

D is for Dahmer

Life: 1960-1994
Cause of Death: Bludgeoning
State: Wisconsin
Victims: 17
Criminal Penalty: 941 yrs in prison

"It's hard for me to believe that a human being could have done what I've done, but I know that I did it."

Jeffrey Dahmer, brought
men home to kill,
and kept their remains with a
twisted thrill.
He killed and ate them until
the very end.
Police should have listened to
Glenda Cleveland.

Ed Gein was mean,
A grave robbing machine.
He would've liked to wear your face.
The man was a disgrace!

"I didn't want to hurt them, I only wanted to possess them."

E is for Ed Gein

Life: 1906-1984
Cause of Death: Lung Cancer
State: Wisconsin
Victims: 2 murders confirmed, 7 others suspected, 9 corpses desecrated
Criminal Penalty: 6 Death Sentences

"I like children, they are tasty."

Albert Fish had a wish.
Little girls were his favorite dish.
"Ham & Eggs" would've been more fair.
Thanksfully, he was scrambled by the electric chair.

Many may think that clowns are the worst.
In a game of bad clowns, John Wayne Gacy takes first.
He lured young boys to his home to slay.
And half-buried their bodies in a gruesome display.

G is for Gacy

Life: 1942-1994
Execution: Lethal Injection
States: Illinois, Iowa
Victims: 33+
Criminal Penalty: Death

H is for H. H. Holmes

Life: 1861-1896
Execution: Hanged
State: Florida
Victims: 1-9+
Criminal Penalty: 6 Death Sentences

Herman Webster Mudgett
was assuredly a prick.
Built a hotel in Chicago, and
the reason is sick.
Away from his wife and child
he did walk,
then murdered the guests;
his name stolen from
Sherlock.

"I was born with the devil in me."

Ivan Milat is dead, his reign of terror done.
Seven backpackers he killed, one by one.
In the Belanglo State Forest, he lured them in,
and left their families to mourn as he wickedly grinned.

I is for Ivan

Life: 1944-2019
Cause of Death: Stomach Cancer
Country: Australia
Victims: 7+
Criminal Penalty: 7 Life Sentences

J is for Jablonski

Life: 1946-2019
Cause of Death: Unknown
State: California, Utah
Victims: 5
Criminal Penalty: 6 Death Sentences

Phillip Carl Jablonski, a killer so cold,
took five women's lives, maybe more, we are told.
For some odd reason, they kept letting him out.
Now dead, but he used to write poems for clout.

"Allow me to introduce myself as Death Row Teddy."

A killer at 15, his name was
Edmund Kemper.
Tall and disgusting, with one
hell of a temper.
"Wanted to see what it felt like
to kill grandma," he said.
Not to mention what he did
to his own mother's head.
(Whoops!)

"It's not easy. Butchering people is hard work. Physically and mentally. I don't think people realize you need to vent."

K is for Kemper

Life: 1945-Present
Imprisoned at: California Medical
Country: California
Victims: 10
Criminal Penalty: Life Imprsonment

L is for Leonard Lake

Life: 1945-1985
Cause of Death: Suicide by Cyanide
State: California
Victims: 11 confirmed, 25 suspected

Charles NG: 1960-Present
Imprisoned at: San Quentin State
Criminal Penalty: Lethal Injection

Leonard Lake and
Charles Ng, a duo so
vile,
built a torture
bunker where they
killed with a smile.
They kidnapped and
murdered, with no
remorse.
Their crimes and
videos, a chilling
discourse.

Charles Manson, a cult leader so insane,
he convinced "The Family" to kill without refrain.
He orchestrated multiple murders with glee.
His legacy of evil will forever be.

"You people would convict a grilled cheese sandwhich of murder and noone would question it."

M is for Manson

Life: 1934-2017
Cause of Death: Colon Cancer
State: California
Victims: 9+ Murdered by proxy
Criminal Penalty: Death; commuted to life imprisonment

N is for Nannie Doss

Life: 1905-1965
Cause of Death: Leukemia
States: Alabama, NC, Kansas, OK
Victims: 11
Criminal Penalty: Life Imprisonment

Nannie Doss, also known as the "giggling granny," four husbands among those she killed, which were many.
With rat poison she shockingly took all their lives.
All left behind a long and violent trail of lies.

"I was searching for the perfect mate."

Otis Toole, a drifter so wild,
killed and burned, like a demon defiled.
He confessed to crimes, but which ones were true?
The mystery remains...
a chilling residue.

"I ate a little bit of him."

O is for Otis

Life: 1947-1996
Cause of Death: Cirrhosis
States: Michigan, Florida, Texas
Victims: 6 confirmed, 1 suspected, hundreds claimed
Criminal Penalty: 6 Death Sentences

P is for Puente

Life: 1929-2011
Cause of Death: Natural Causes
State: California
Victims: 9
Criminal Penalty: Life Imprisonment

Dorothea Puente, a landlady less than sweet,
but beneath the surface, a killer did greet.
She poisoned her boarders then buried them deep.
Puente's house of horrors, where evil did creep.

"I don't feel like confessing my sins to anyone."

Wang Qiang took 45 lives.
Executed November
2005.
He assaulted and
murdered, without a care.
Leaving a trail of horror,
too much to bear.

Q is for Qiang

Born: 1975
Executed: 2005
Country: China
Victims: 45+
Criminal Penalty: Death

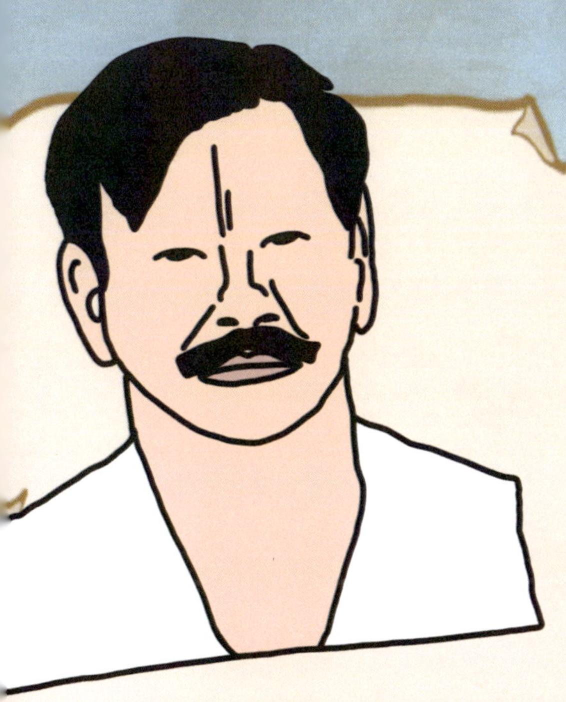

R is for Ridgeway

Gary Ridgeway, Green River
Killer of hate,
took 49 lives up in
Washington state.

*"I hate the whole damned human race,
including myself."*

R is also for Ramirez

Below in LA, Richard
Ramirez stalked the night,
until 2013, when blood
cancer ended his fight.

*"Fear is my weapon, and I wield it
with deadly precision."*

Sentenced to 2410 years, no chance of parole,
thus I appropriately rename him Moses SHIThole.
Murdered 38 women and 1 toddler in a field,
The ABC Murderer, his fate is sealed.

"Hurt has been my daily bread."

S is for Sithole

Life: 1964-Present
Imprisoned at: C-Max
Country: South Africa
Victims: 38 confirmed, 76 suspected
Criminal Penalty: 2,410 yrs in prison

T is for Ted Bundy

Life: 1946-1989
Execution: Electric Chair
States: CA, CO, FL, ID, OR, UT, WA
Victims: 7
Criminal Penalty: Death

"I'm the most cold-hearted son-of-a-bitch you'll ever meet."

Charismatic, cunning, some
said handsome, yet strange
Ted Bundy had many support-
ers (all deranged!)
Thirty plus victims, he visited
in the wood.
A sadistic sociopath, always
up to no good.

William Unek, a constable vile,
killed 57 people, with a
creepy-ass smile.
He use an axe, a knife, and a
gun.
A legacy of evil, thankfully
undone.

U is for Unek

Life: 1929-1957
Execution: Severe burns from smoke
bomb thrown by police
Country: Belgian Congo
Victims: 57 killed, 30+ injured

V is for Vera

Life: 1903-1960
End of Life: Delirium and Amnesia
Country: Romania
Victims: 35
Criminal Penalty: Life Imprisonment

Vera Renczi, a killer so sly, poisoned her victims, with no alibi.
She took 35 lives, with arsenic green.
A chilling tale of a woman so mean.

"I could not endure the thought that they would ever put their arms around another woman after they had embraced me."

William Bonin, dropped out of a high school.
Killed 21 boys from Cali... not cool!
The first to die by lethal injection.
He was a sexual psychopath from lifelong rejection.

"When a person has a thought of doing anything serious against the law...they should go to a quiet place and think about it seriously."

W is for William

Life: 1947-1996
Execution: Lethal Injection
State: California
Victims: 21-36+
Criminal Penalty: Death

Execution: Hanging in 1960
Country: South African Union
Victims: 16
Criminal Penalty: Death

Elias Xitavhudzi, Pangaman
he was named.
A machete his weapon, he
victims weere mained.
Sixteen women he killed, in
Atterridgeville town.
Justice was served, he was
hanged then thrown down.

Father, husband, teacher, pilot.
Robert Lee Yates was awfully violent.
Sixteen women he killed, mostly prostitutes.
His killing spree ended, his fate absolute.

Y is for Yates

Life: 1952-
Imprisoned at: Washington State Pen.
State: Washington
Victims: 16+
Criminal Penalty: 408 yrs. and Death

Z is for Zodiac

Criminal Status: Unidentified
States: California, Nevada
Victims: 5 confirmed, 2 injured,
possibly 20-28 total
Never Caught

The Zodiac Killer, a mystery unsolved.
His taunting letters are a story untold.
Five victims confirmed, his identity unknown,
a cipher cracked, but his true self not shown.

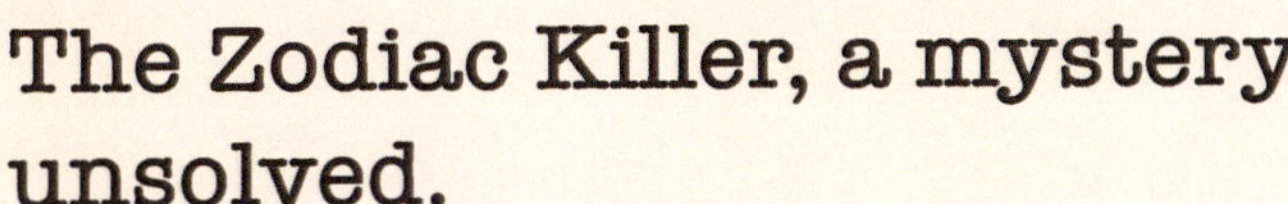

"I like killing people because it is so much fun. It is more fun than killing wild game in the forest because man is the most dangerous animals of them all."

REMEMBERING THE VICTIMS

Richard Mallory
David Spears
Charles Carskaddon
Peter Siems
Troy Burress
Charles Humphreys
Walter Antonio
Donna Lauria
Jody Valenti
Carl Denaro
Rosemary Keenan
Donna DeMasi
Joanne Lomino
Christine Freund
John Diel
Virginia Voskerichian
Stacy Moskowitz
Robert Warnke
John Moore
Bushart
George Henry McMahon
Alexander Luszzock
Alexander Uszacke
Curtis Straughter
Steven Mark Hicks
Richard Guerrero
Jeremy Weinberger
Jamie Doxtator
Ricky Beeks
Oliver Lacy
Errol Lindsey
Konerak Sinthasomphone
Ernest Miller
Anthony Hughes
Joseph Bradehoft

Matt Turner
Anthony Sears
David C. Thomas
Edward W. Smith
Mary Hogan
Bernice Worden
Grace Budd
William E. "Billy" Gaffney
Francis J. McDonnell
Emma Richardson
Timothy Jack McCoy
John Butkovich
Darrell Julius Samson
Randall Wayne Reffett
Samuel G. Dodd
Stapleton
Michael Lawrence Bonnin
William Huey Carroll Jr.
James Byron Haakenson
Rick Louis Johnston
Kenneth Ray Parker
Michael M. Marino
William George Bundy
Francis Wayne Alexander
Gregory John Godzik
John Alan Szyc
John Steven Prestidge
Matthew Walter Bowman
Robert Edward Gilroy Jr.
John Antheny Mowery
Russell Lloyd Nelson
Robert David Winch
Tommy Joe Boling
David Paul Talsma
William Wayne Kindred
Timothy David O'Rourke

Frank William Landingin
James Mazzara
Robert Jerome Piest
Julia Connor
Pearl Connor
Emeline Cigrand
Minni Williams
Nannie Williams
Ben Pitezel
Howard Pitezel
Alice Pitezel
Nellie Pitezel
James Gibson
Deborah Everist
Simone Schmidl
Anja Habschied
Gabor Neugebauer
Caroline Clarke
Joanne Walters
Linda Kimball
Carol Spadoni
Eva Peterson
Fathyma Vann
Margie Rogers
Maude M. Hughey Kemper
Edmund Emil Kemper Sr.
Mary Ann Pesce
Anita Luchessa
Aiko Koo
Cindy Schall
Rosalind Thorpe
Alice Liu
Clarnell Strandberg
Sally (Sara) Hallett
Harvey, Deborah, Sean Dubbs

Melanie Cooley
Lynette Culver
Susan Curtis
Margaret Bowman
Lisa Levy
Kathy Kleiner
Karen Chandler
Cheryl Thomas
Kimberly Leach
Karl Schick
Lorenzo Schick
Milorad
David Faraday
Betty Lou Jensen
Darlene Ferrin
Mike Mageau
Cecelia Shepard
Bryan Hartnell
Paul Stine
Ray Davis
Cheri Jo Bates

Lonnie, Brenda, & Lonnoie Jr. Bond
Kathleen Allen
Michael Carroll
Robin Stapley
Randy Johnson
Charles Gunnar
Donald Lake
Paul Cosner
Sharon Tate
Jay Sebring
Voytek Frykowski
Abigail Folger
Steven Parent
Leno LaBianca
Rosemary LaBianca
Gary Hinman
Donald "Shorty" Shea
Zelmer Braggs
Gertrude Braggs
Robert Lee Haynes
Frank Harrelson
Arlie Lanning
Dovie Weaver
Richard L. Morton
Samuel Doss
Adam Walsh
George Sonnenberg
David Schallart
Ada Johnson
Ruth Monroe
Everson Theodore Gillmouth
Betty Mae Palmer
Leona Carpenter
James Gallop
Eugene Gamel
Vera Faye Martin
Dorothy Miller
Alvaro "Bert" Gonzales Montoya

Benjamin Fink
Weny Lee Coffield
Gisele Ann Lovvorn
Debra Lynn Bonner
Marcia Fay Chapman
Opal Charmaine Mills
Terry Rene Milligan
Mary Bridget Meehan
Debra Lorraine Estes
Linda Jane Rule
Denise Darcel Bush
Shawnda Leea Summers
Shirley Marie Sherrill
Colleen Renee
Andrea M. Childers
Sandra Kay Gabbert
Kimi-Kai Pitsor
Marie M. Malvar
Carol Ann Christensen
Martina Theresa Authoriee
Cheryl Lee Wims
Yvonne Shelly Antosh
Carrie A. Rois
Constance Elizabeth Naon
Debbie May Abernathy
Tracy Ann Winston
Maureen Sue Feeney
Mary Sue Bello
Pammy Avent
Delise Louise Plager
Kimberly Nelson
Lisa Yates
Mary Exzetta West
Cindy Anne Smith
Patricia Michelle Barczak
Robert Joseph Hayes
Marta Reeves
Patricia Yellowrobe

Rebecca Marrero
Mei Leung
Jennie Vincow
Dayle Yoshie Okazaki
Tsai-Lian "Veronica" Yu
Vincent Charles Zazzara
Maxine Levenia Zazzara
Bill Doi
Mabel "Ma" Bell
Florence "Nettie" Lang
Carol Kyle
Mary Louise Cannon
Whitney Bennett
Joyce Lucille Nelson
Maxon and Lela Kneiding
Chainaron Khovananth
Somkid Khovananth
Christopher& Virginia Peterson
Sakina and Elyas Abowath
Peter and Barbara Pan
Bill Carns and Inez Erikson
Joni Lenz
Lynda Ann Healy
Donna Gail Mason
Susan Rancourt
Roberta Parks
Brenda Carol Ball
Georgeann Hawkins
Denise Naslund
Janice Ott
Nancy Wilcox
Melissa Smith
Laura Aime
Carol DaRonch
Debra Kent
Caryn Campbell
Julie Cunningham
Denise Oliverson

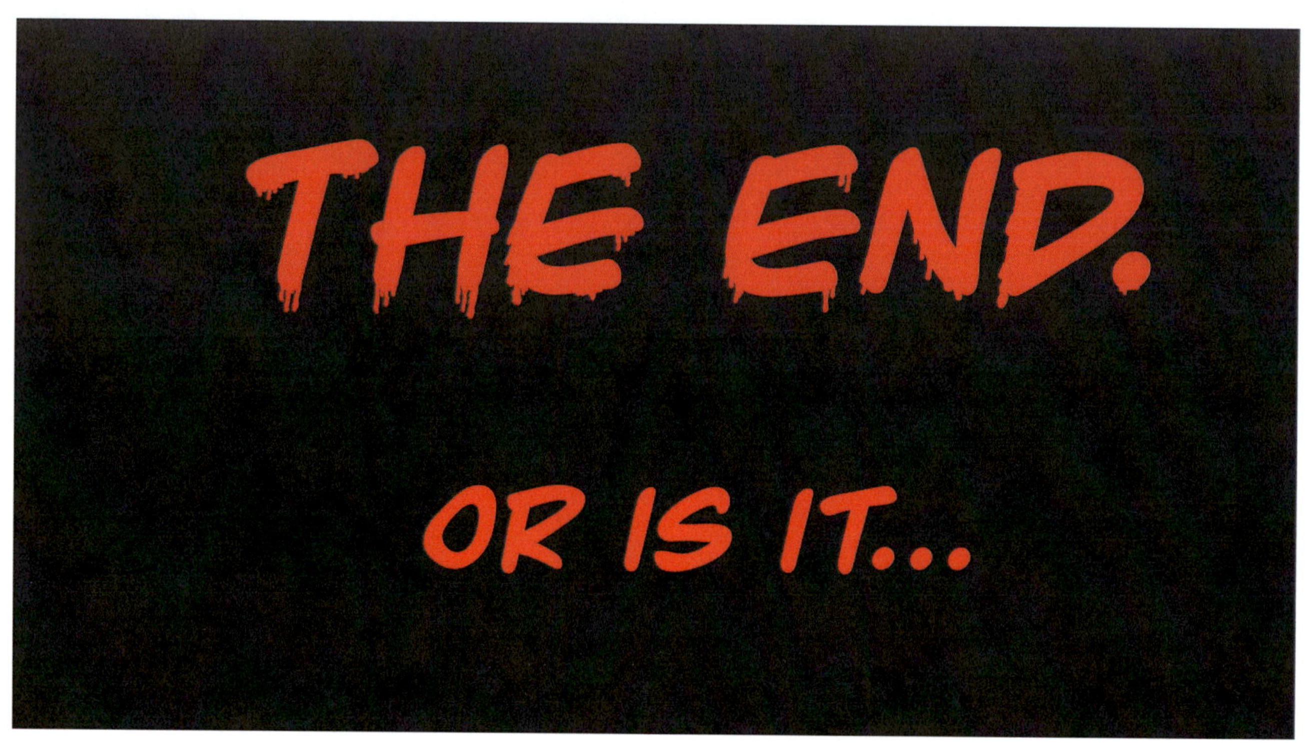

Have fun deciphering the secret anagram hidden within this book...it will reveal what fun Little Lestrange is cooking up next!

-Marie